D1295425

GHOSTLY GRAPHIC ADVENTURES

THE LIGHTHOUSE OF TERROR

Written by Baron Specter
Illustrated by Dustin Evans

visit us at www.abdopublishing.com

Published by Magic Wagon, a division of the ABDO Group, 8000 West 78th Street, Edina, Minnesota 55439. Copyright © 2011 by Abdo Consulting Group, Inc. International copyrights reserved in all countries.
Graphic Planet™ is a trademark and logo of Magic Wagon.

Printed in the United States of America, North Mankato, Minnesota.
042010
092010
♻This book contains at least 10% recycled materials.

Written by Baron Specter
Illustrated by Dustin Evans
Lettered and designed by Ardden Entertainment LLC
Edited by Stephanie Hedlund and Rochelle Baltzer
Cover art by Dustin Evans
Cover design by Ardden Entertainment LLC

Library of Congress Cataloging-in-Publication Data

Specter, Baron, 1957-
  The third adventure : the lighthouse of terror / by Baron Specter ; illustrated by Dustin Evans.
      p. cm. -- (Ghostly graphic adventures)
  Summary: When Joey and friend Gil are caught in a storm while night-fishing off the coast of Massachusetts, they find shelter in a lighthouse inhabited by a very unfriendly ghost.
  ISBN 978-1-60270-772-6
  1. Graphic novels. [1. Graphic novels. 2. Ghosts--Fiction. 3. Time travel--Fiction. 4. Bird Island Light (Mass.)--Fiction. 5. Lighthouses--Fiction. 6. Massachusetts--Fiction.] I. Evans, Dustin, 1982- ill. II. Title. III. Title: Lighthouse of terror.
  PZ7.7.S648Thi 2010
  741.5'973--dc22
                                                            2009052892

TABLE OF CONTENTS

Our Heroes and Villains 4

The Lighthouse of Terror 5

The Bird Island Lighthouse 31

Glossary 32

Web Sites 32

OUR HEROES AND VILLAINS

Gil
Hero

Mr. Jones
Gil's Dad

Joey DeAngelo
Hero

Mrs. Moore
Villain

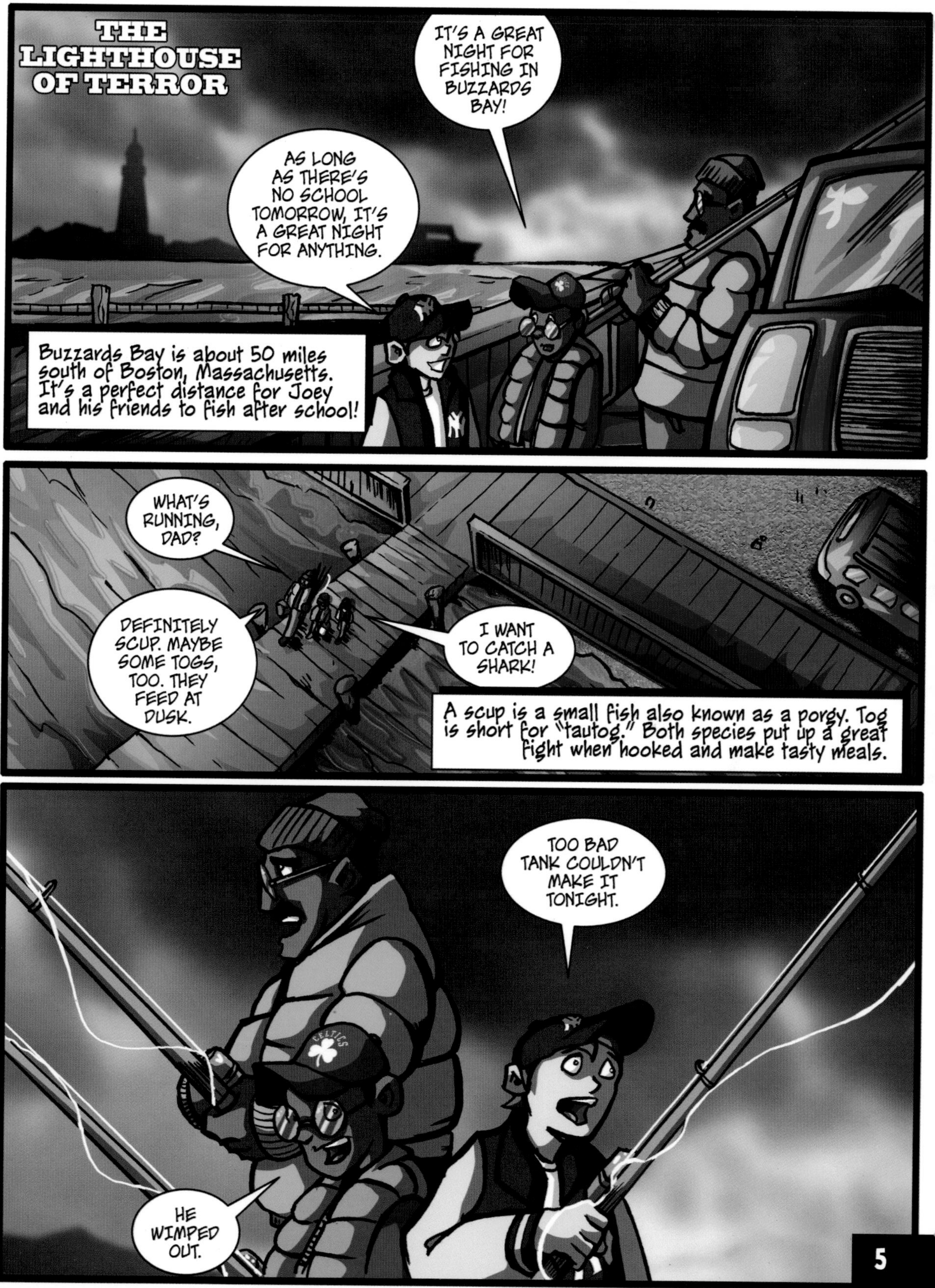
THE LIGHTHOUSE OF TERROR
IT'S A GREAT NIGHT FOR FISHING IN BUZZARDS BAY!
AS LONG AS THERE'S NO SCHOOL TOMORROW, IT'S A GREAT NIGHT FOR ANYTHING.
Buzzards Bay is about 50 miles south of Boston, Massachusetts. It's a perfect distance for Joey and his friends to fish after school!
WHAT'S RUNNING, DAD?
DEFINITELY SCUP. MAYBE SOME TOGS, TOO. THEY FEED AT DUSK.
I WANT TO CATCH A SHARK!
A scup is a small fish also known as a porgy. Tog is short for "tautog." Both species put up a great fight when hooked and make tasty meals.
TOO BAD TANK COULDN'T MAKE IT TONIGHT.
HE WIMPED OUT.

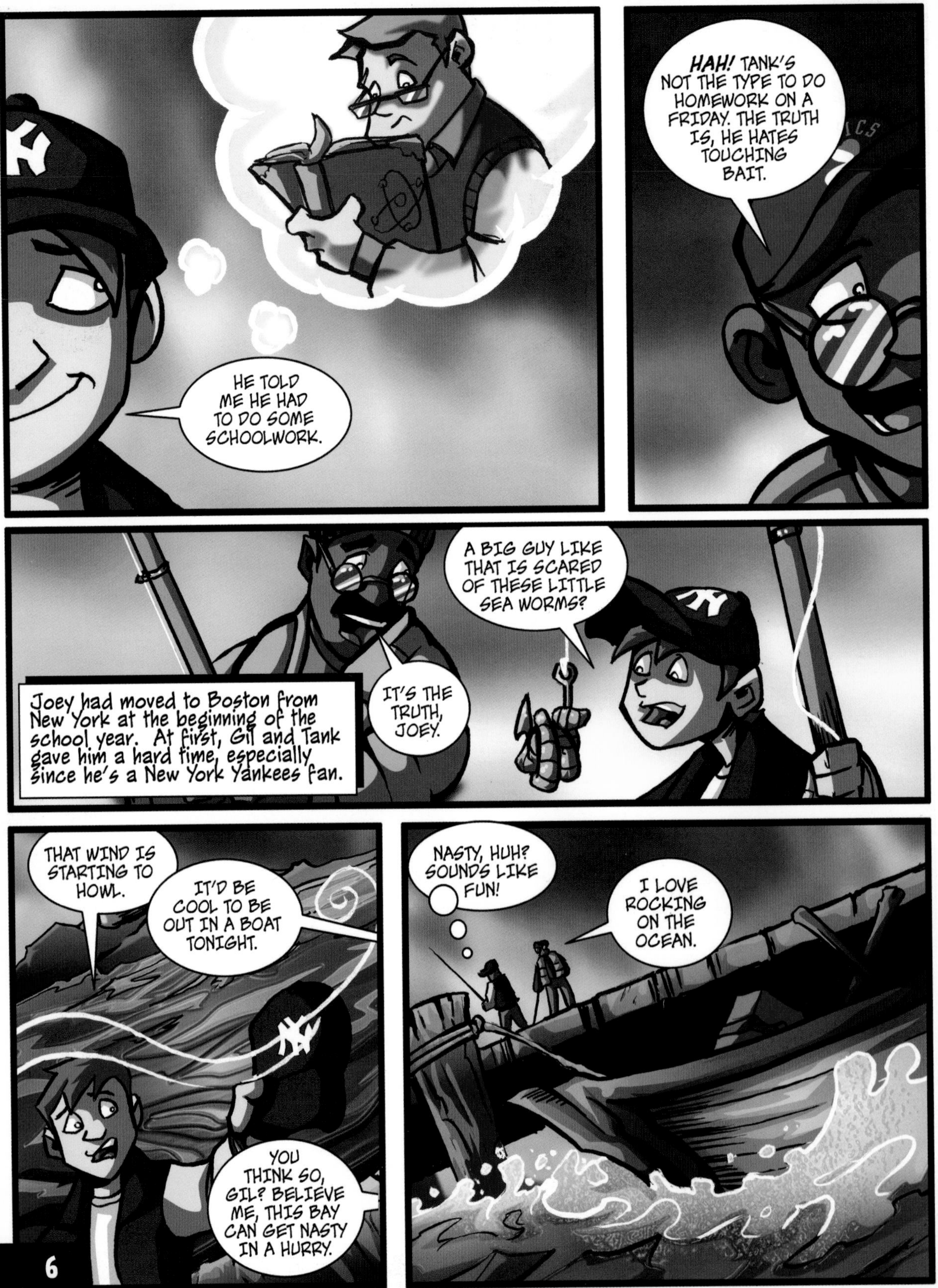
HE TOLD ME HE HAD TO DO SOME SCHOOLWORK.
HAH! TANK'S NOT THE TYPE TO DO HOMEWORK ON A FRIDAY. THE TRUTH IS, HE HATES TOUCHING BAIT.
Joey had moved to Boston from New York at the beginning of the school year. At first, Gil and Tank gave him a hard time, especially since he's a New York Yankees fan.
A BIG GUY LIKE THAT IS SCARED OF THESE LITTLE SEA WORMS?
IT'S THE TRUTH, JOEY.
THAT WIND IS STARTING TO HOWL.
IT'D BE COOL TO BE OUT IN A BOAT TONIGHT.
YOU THINK SO, GIL? BELIEVE ME, THIS BAY CAN GET NASTY IN A HURRY.
NASTY, HUH? SOUNDS LIKE FUN!
I LOVE ROCKING ON THE OCEAN.

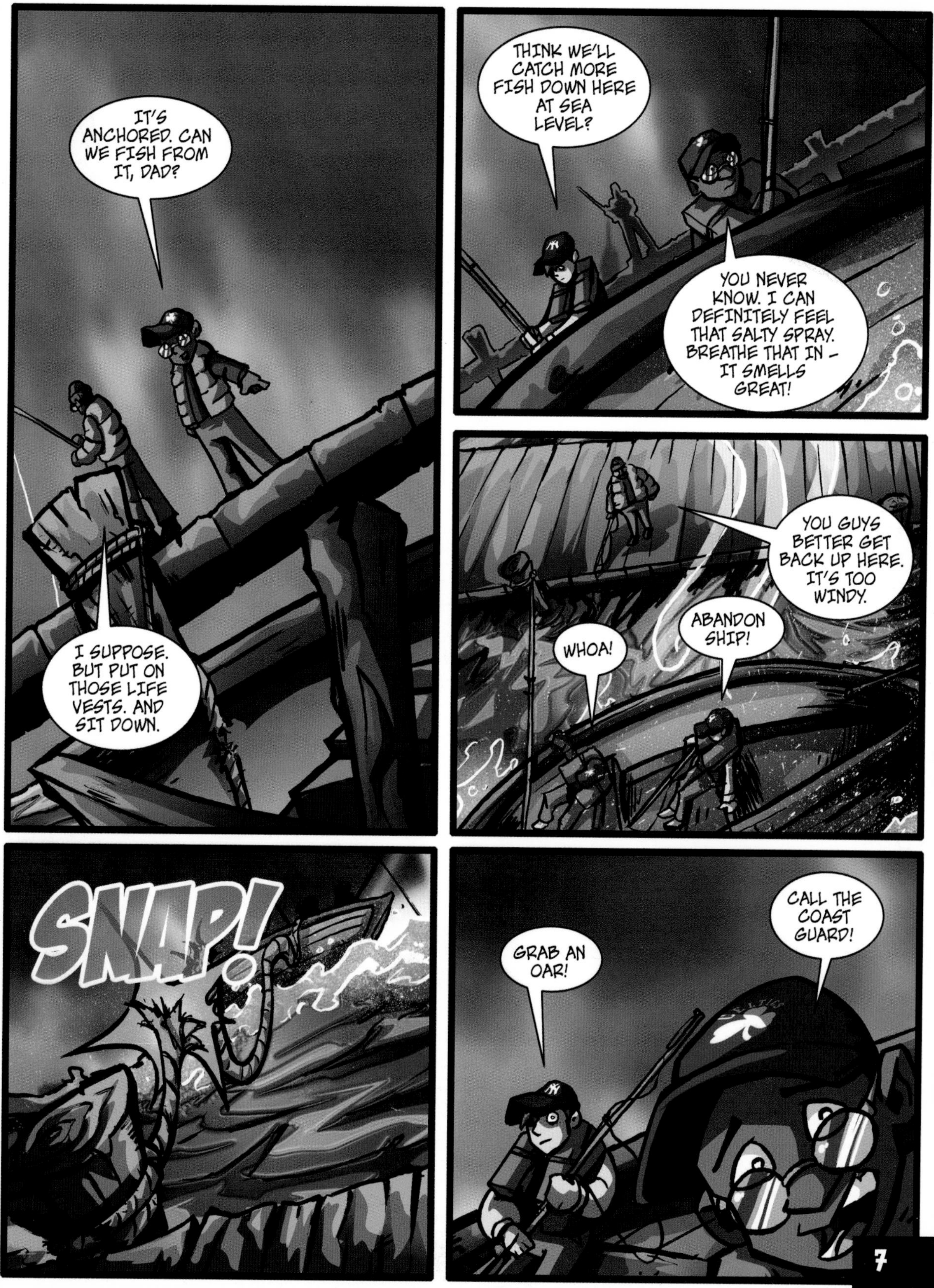
IT'S ANCHORED. CAN WE FISH FROM IT, DAD?
I SUPPOSE. BUT PUT ON THOSE LIFE VESTS. AND SIT DOWN.
THINK WE'LL CATCH MORE FISH DOWN HERE AT SEA LEVEL?
YOU NEVER KNOW. I CAN DEFINITELY FEEL THAT SALTY SPRAY. BREATHE THAT IN – IT SMELLS GREAT!
YOU GUYS BETTER GET BACK UP HERE. IT'S TOO WINDY.
WHOA!
ABANDON SHIP!
SNAP!
GRAB AN OAR!
CALL THE COAST GUARD!

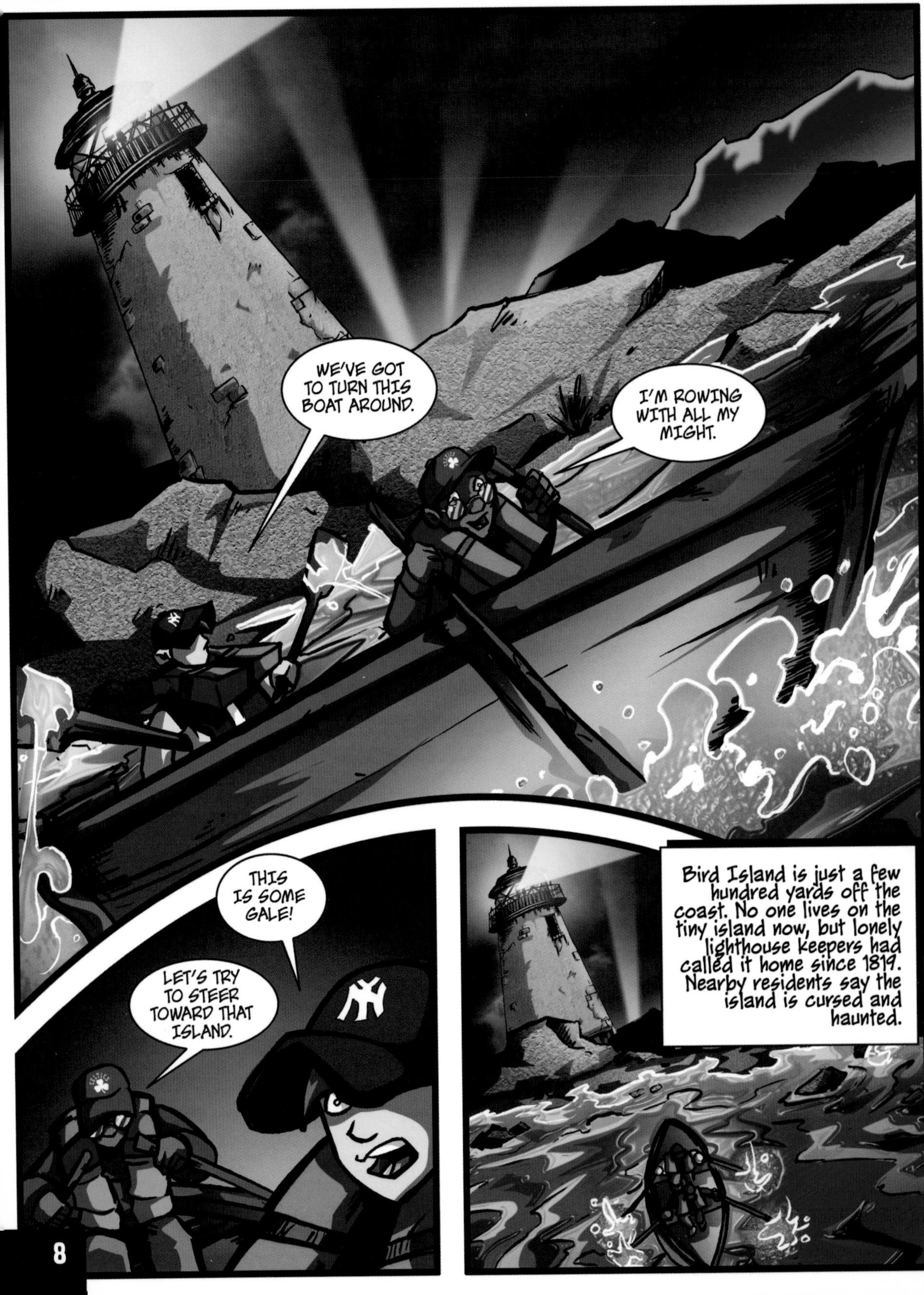
WE'VE GOT TO TURN THIS BOAT AROUND.
I'M ROWING WITH ALL MY MIGHT.
THIS IS SOME GALE!
LET'S TRY TO STEER TOWARD THAT ISLAND.
Bird Island is just a few hundred yards off the coast. No one lives on the tiny island now, but lonely lighthouse keepers had called it home since 1819. Nearby residents say the island is cursed and haunted.

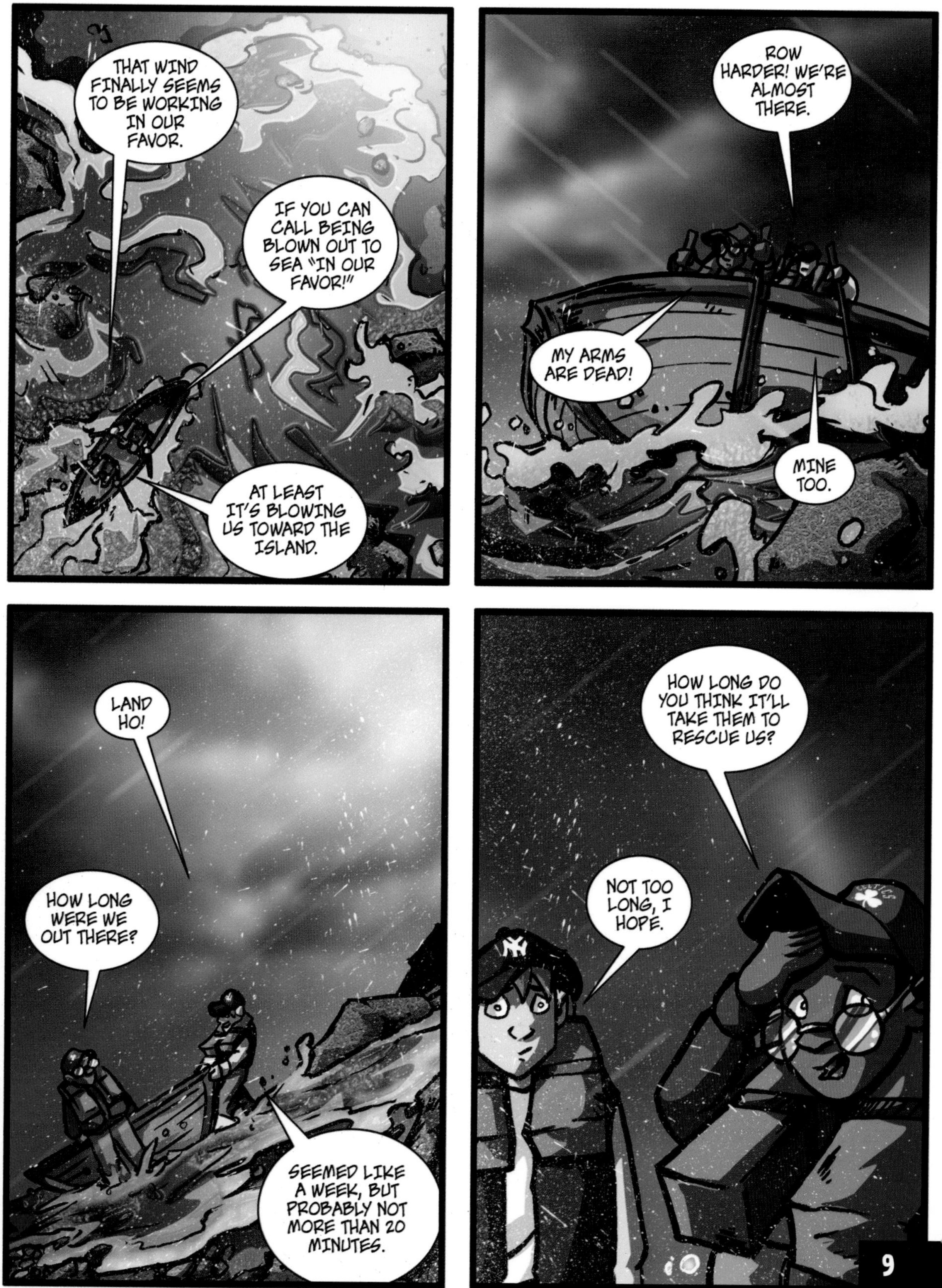
THAT WIND FINALLY SEEMS TO BE WORKING IN OUR FAVOR.
IF YOU CAN CALL BEING BLOWN OUT TO SEA "IN OUR FAVOR!"
AT LEAST IT'S BLOWING US TOWARD THE ISLAND.
ROW HARDER! WE'RE ALMOST THERE.
MY ARMS ARE DEAD!
MINE TOO.
LAND HO!
HOW LONG WERE WE OUT THERE?
SEEMED LIKE A WEEK, BUT PROBABLY NOT MORE THAN 20 MINUTES.
HOW LONG DO YOU THINK IT'LL TAKE THEM TO RESCUE US?
NOT TOO LONG, I HOPE.

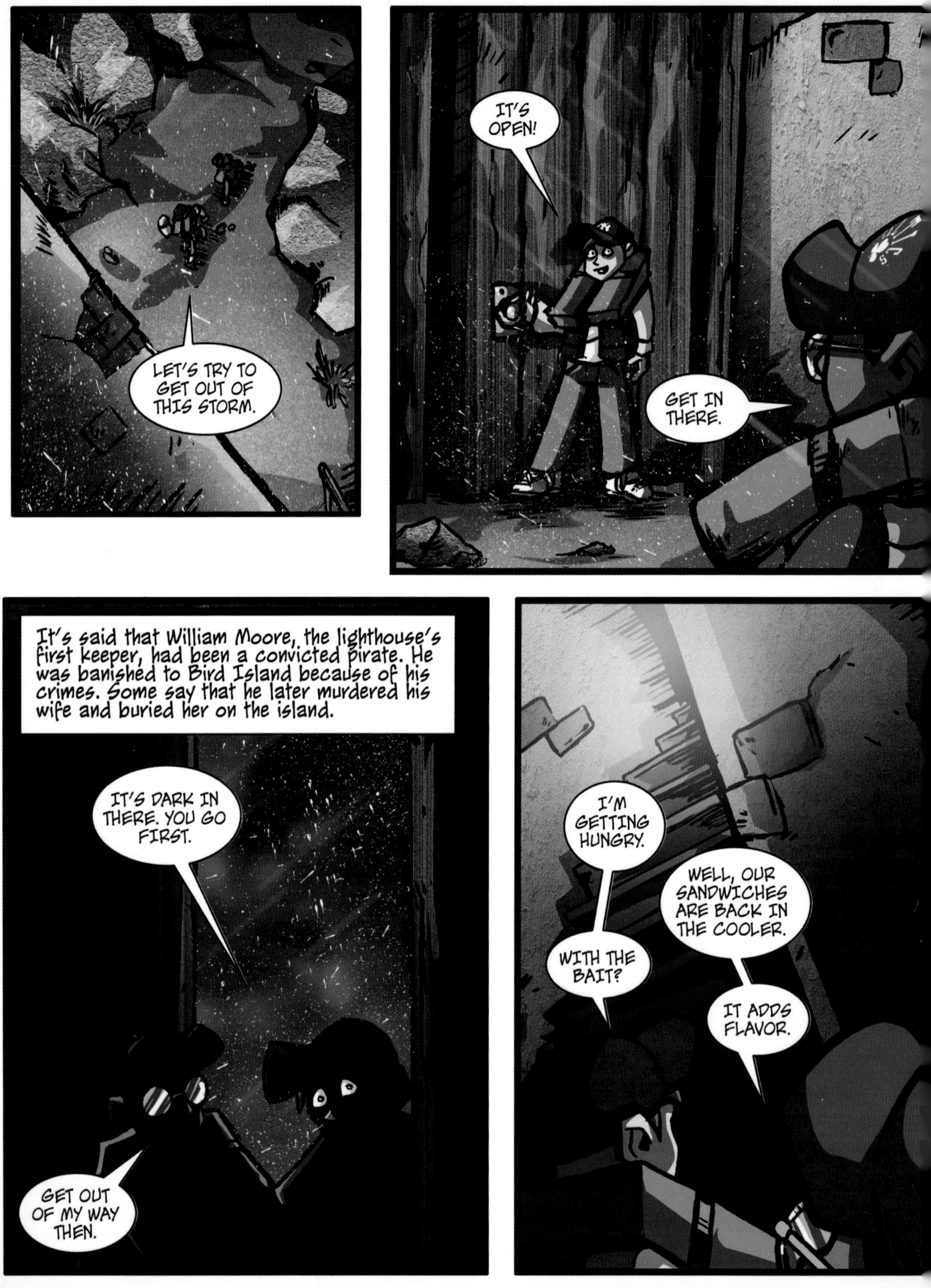
LET'S TRY TO GET OUT OF THIS STORM.
IT'S OPEN!
GET IN THERE.
It's said that William Moore, the lighthouse's first keeper, had been a convicted pirate. He was banished to Bird Island because of his crimes. Some say that he later murdered his wife and buried her on the island.
IT'S DARK IN THERE. YOU GO FIRST.
GET OUT OF MY WAY THEN.
I'M GETTING HUNGRY.
WELL, OUR SANDWICHES ARE BACK IN THE COOLER.
WITH THE BAIT?
IT ADDS FLAVOR.

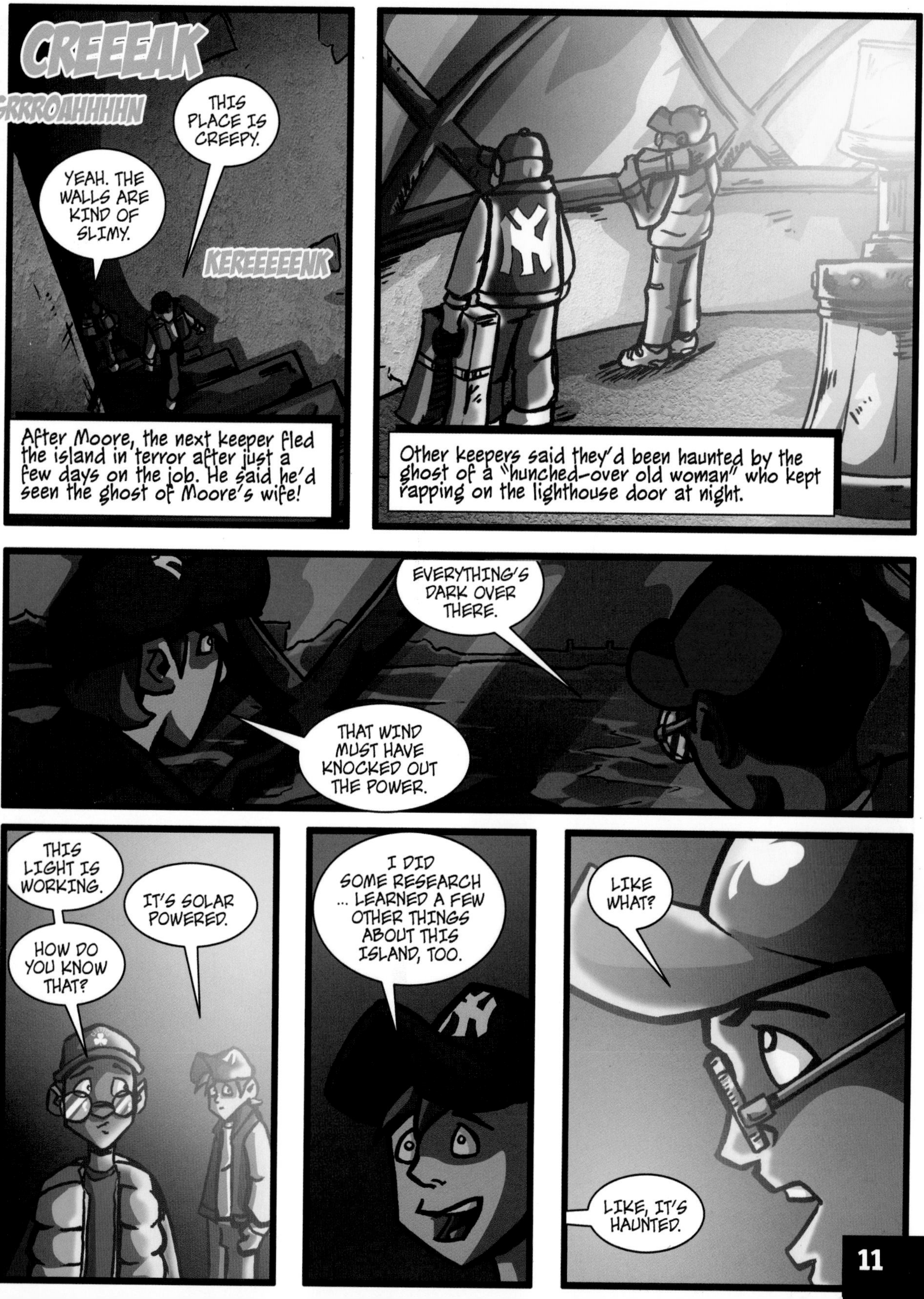
CREEEAK
GRRROAHHHHN
THIS PLACE IS CREEPY.
YEAH. THE WALLS ARE KIND OF SLIMY.
KEREEEEENK
After Moore, the next keeper fled the island in terror after just a few days on the job. He said he'd seen the ghost of Moore's wife!
Other keepers said they'd been haunted by the ghost of a "hunched-over old woman" who kept rapping on the lighthouse door at night.
EVERYTHING'S DARK OVER THERE.
THAT WIND MUST HAVE KNOCKED OUT THE POWER.
THIS LIGHT IS WORKING.
IT'S SOLAR POWERED.
HOW DO YOU KNOW THAT?
I DID SOME RESEARCH ... LEARNED A FEW OTHER THINGS ABOUT THIS ISLAND, TOO.
LIKE WHAT?
LIKE, IT'S HAUNTED.

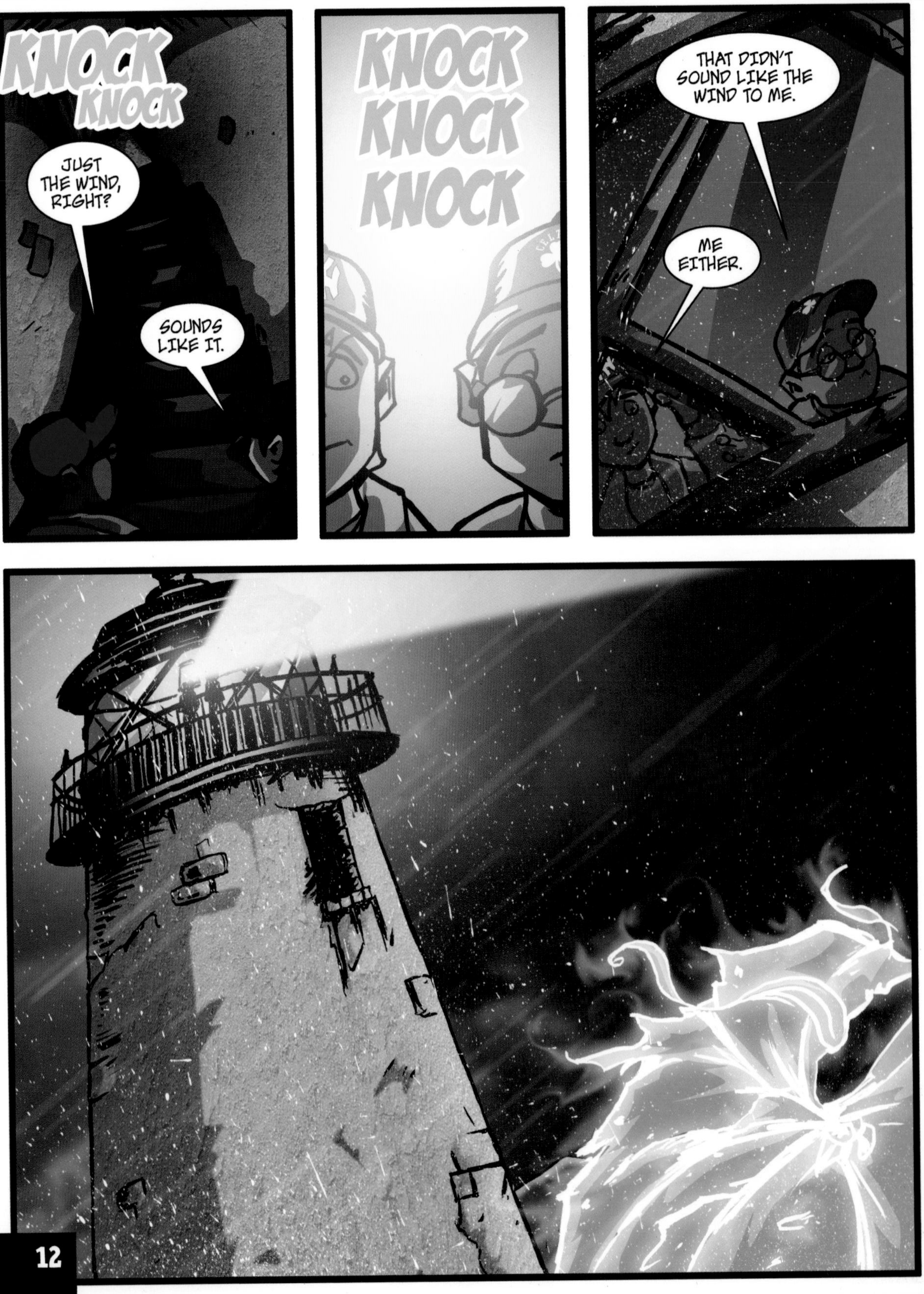
KNOCK KNOCK
JUST THE WIND, RIGHT?
SOUNDS LIKE IT.
KNOCK KNOCK KNOCK
THAT DIDN'T SOUND LIKE THE WIND TO ME.
ME EITHER.

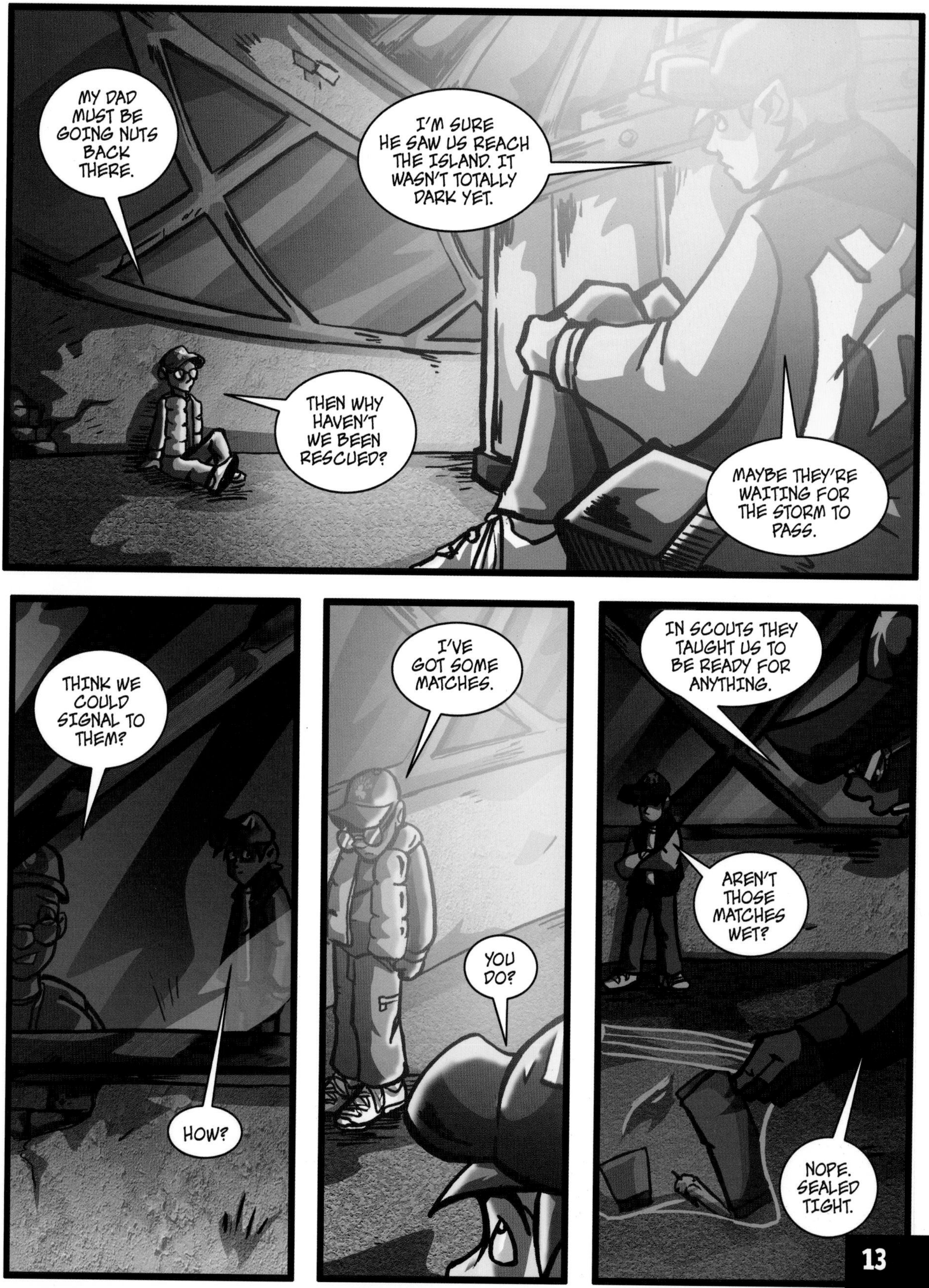
MY DAD MUST BE GOING NUTS BACK THERE.
I'M SURE HE SAW US REACH THE ISLAND. IT WASN'T TOTALLY DARK YET.
THEN WHY HAVEN'T WE BEEN RESCUED?
MAYBE THEY'RE WAITING FOR THE STORM TO PASS.
THINK WE COULD SIGNAL TO THEM?
HOW?
I'VE GOT SOME MATCHES.
YOU DO?
IN SCOUTS THEY TAUGHT US TO BE READY FOR ANYTHING.
AREN'T THOSE MATCHES WET?
NOPE. SEALED TIGHT.

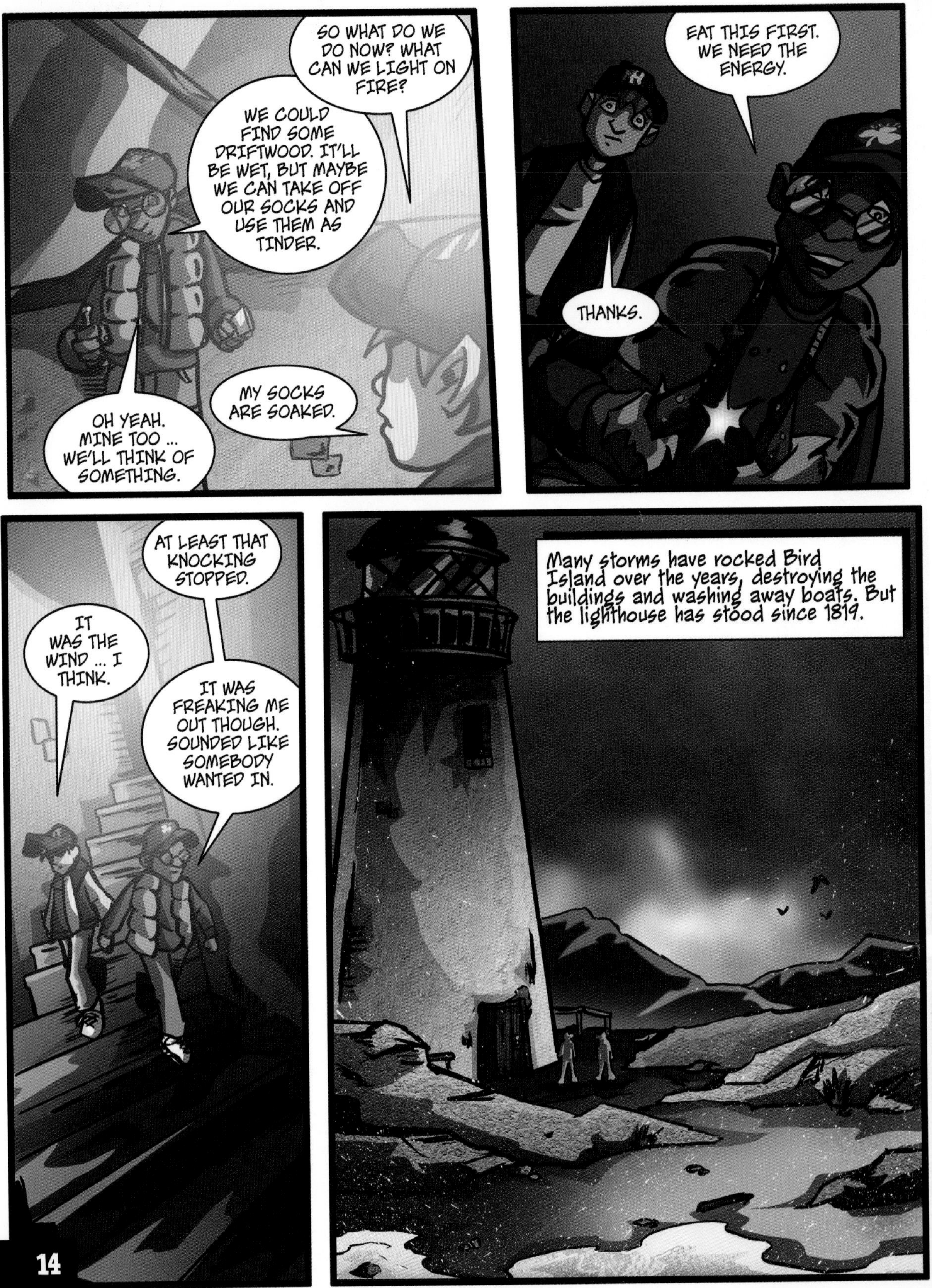
SO WHAT DO WE DO NOW? WHAT CAN WE LIGHT ON FIRE?
WE COULD FIND SOME DRIFTWOOD. IT'LL BE WET, BUT MAYBE WE CAN TAKE OFF OUR SOCKS AND USE THEM AS TINDER.
MY SOCKS ARE SOAKED.
OH YEAH. MINE TOO ... WE'LL THINK OF SOMETHING.
EAT THIS FIRST. WE NEED THE ENERGY.
THANKS.
AT LEAST THAT KNOCKING STOPPED.
IT WAS THE WIND ... I THINK.
IT WAS FREAKING ME OUT THOUGH. SOUNDED LIKE SOMEBODY WANTED IN.
Many storms have rocked Bird Island over the years, destroying the buildings and washing away boats. But the lighthouse has stood since 1819.

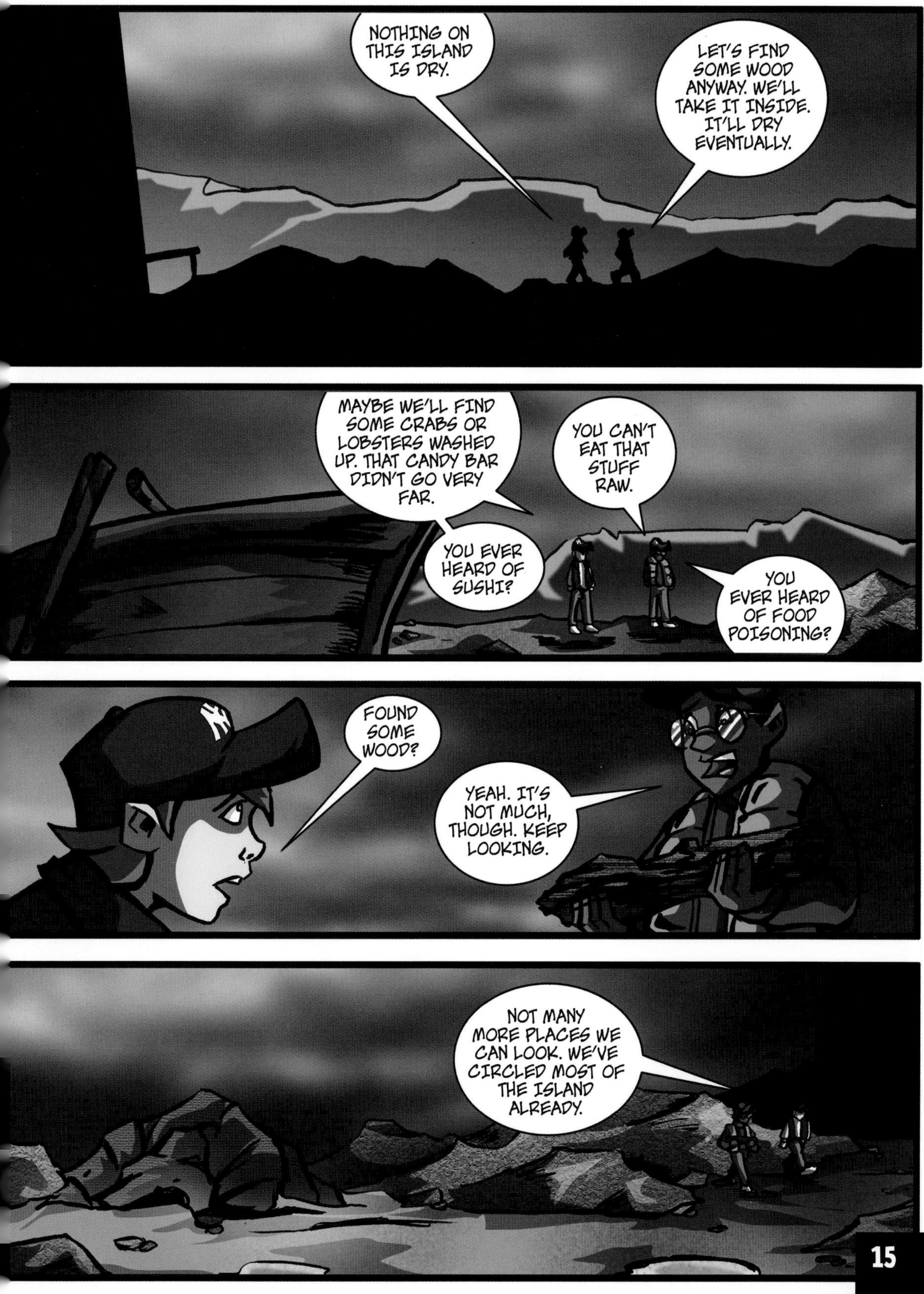
NOTHING ON THIS ISLAND IS DRY.
LET'S FIND SOME WOOD ANYWAY. WE'LL TAKE IT INSIDE. IT'LL DRY EVENTUALLY.
MAYBE WE'LL FIND SOME CRABS OR LOBSTERS WASHED UP. THAT CANDY BAR DIDN'T GO VERY FAR.
YOU CAN'T EAT THAT STUFF RAW.
YOU EVER HEARD OF SUSHI?
YOU EVER HEARD OF FOOD POISONING?
FOUND SOME WOOD?
YEAH. IT'S NOT MUCH, THOUGH. KEEP LOOKING.
NOT MANY MORE PLACES WE CAN LOOK. WE'VE CIRCLED MOST OF THE ISLAND ALREADY.

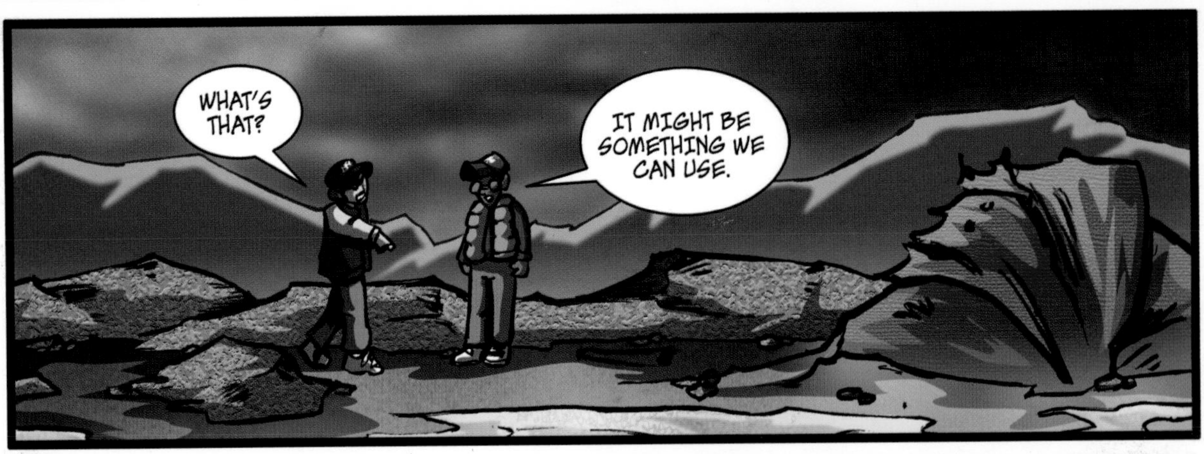
WHAT'S THAT?
IT MIGHT BE SOMETHING WE CAN USE.

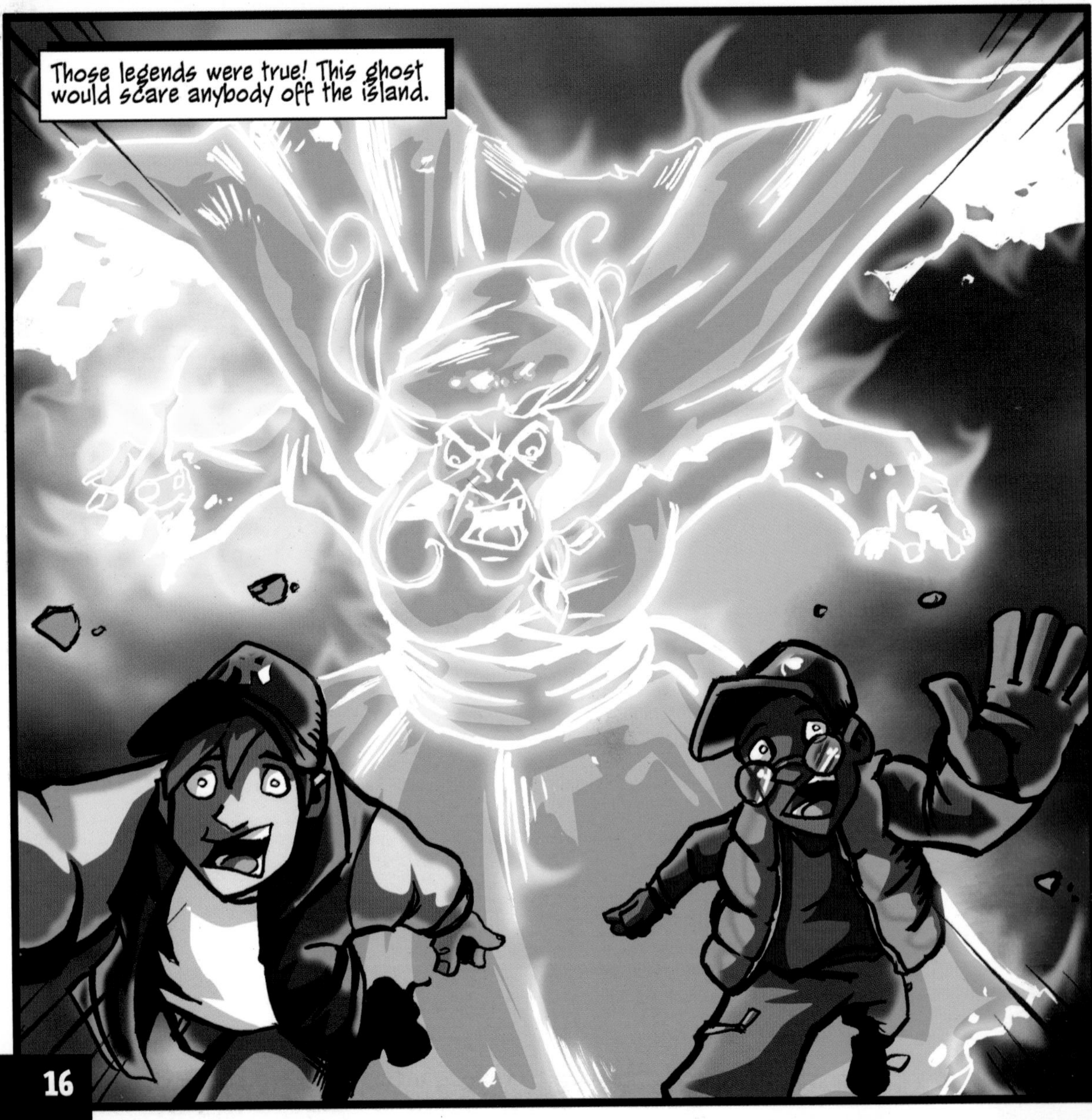
Those legends were true! This ghost would scare anybody off the island.

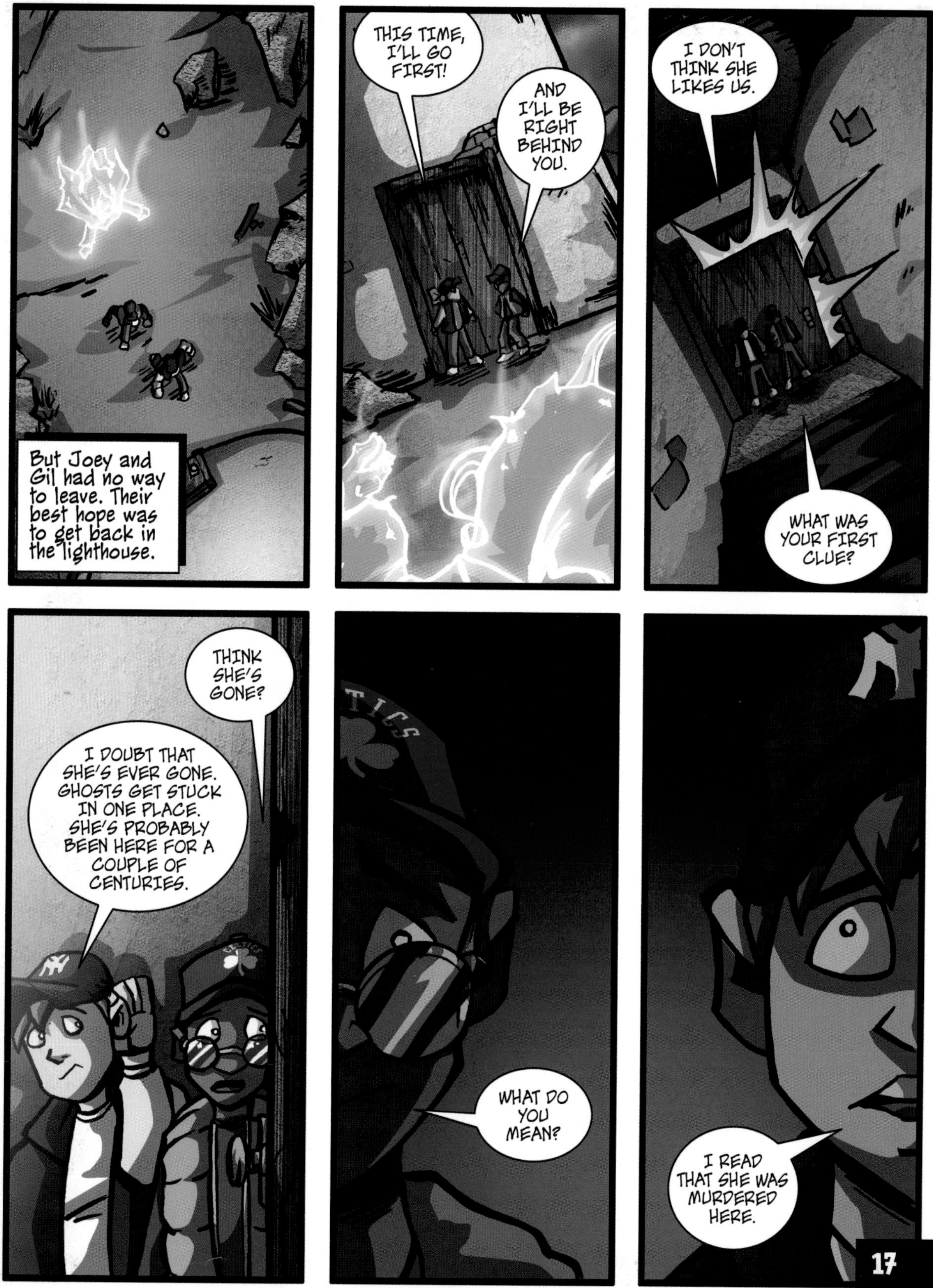
But Joey and Gil had no way to leave. Their best hope was to get back in the lighthouse.
THIS TIME, I'LL GO FIRST!
AND I'LL BE RIGHT BEHIND YOU.
I DON'T THINK SHE LIKES US.
WHAT WAS YOUR FIRST CLUE?
THINK SHE'S GONE?
I DOUBT THAT SHE'S EVER GONE. GHOSTS GET STUCK IN ONE PLACE. SHE'S PROBABLY BEEN HERE FOR A COUPLE OF CENTURIES.
WHAT DO YOU MEAN?
I READ THAT SHE WAS MURDERED HERE.

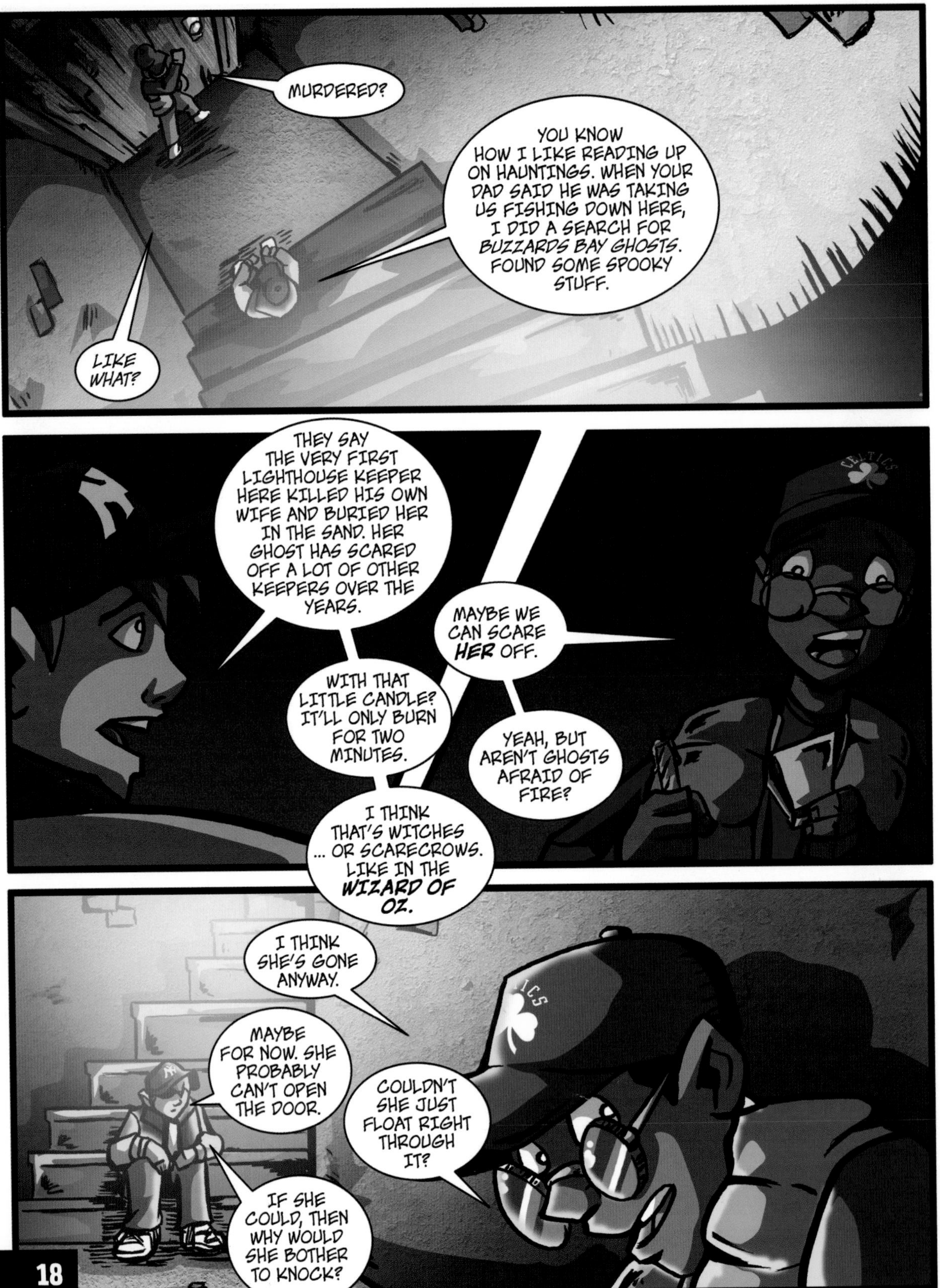
MURDERED?
YOU KNOW HOW I LIKE READING UP ON HAUNTINGS. WHEN YOUR DAD SAID HE WAS TAKING US FISHING DOWN HERE, I DID A SEARCH FOR BUZZARDS BAY GHOSTS. FOUND SOME SPOOKY STUFF.
LIKE WHAT?
THEY SAY THE VERY FIRST LIGHTHOUSE KEEPER HERE KILLED HIS OWN WIFE AND BURIED HER IN THE SAND. HER GHOST HAS SCARED OFF A LOT OF OTHER KEEPERS OVER THE YEARS.
MAYBE WE CAN SCARE HER OFF.
WITH THAT LITTLE CANDLE? IT'LL ONLY BURN FOR TWO MINUTES.
YEAH, BUT AREN'T GHOSTS AFRAID OF FIRE?
I THINK THAT'S WITCHES ... OR SCARECROWS. LIKE IN THE WIZARD OF OZ.
I THINK SHE'S GONE ANYWAY.
MAYBE FOR NOW. SHE PROBABLY CAN'T OPEN THE DOOR.
COULDN'T SHE JUST FLOAT RIGHT THROUGH IT?
IF SHE COULD, THEN WHY WOULD SHE BOTHER TO KNOCK?

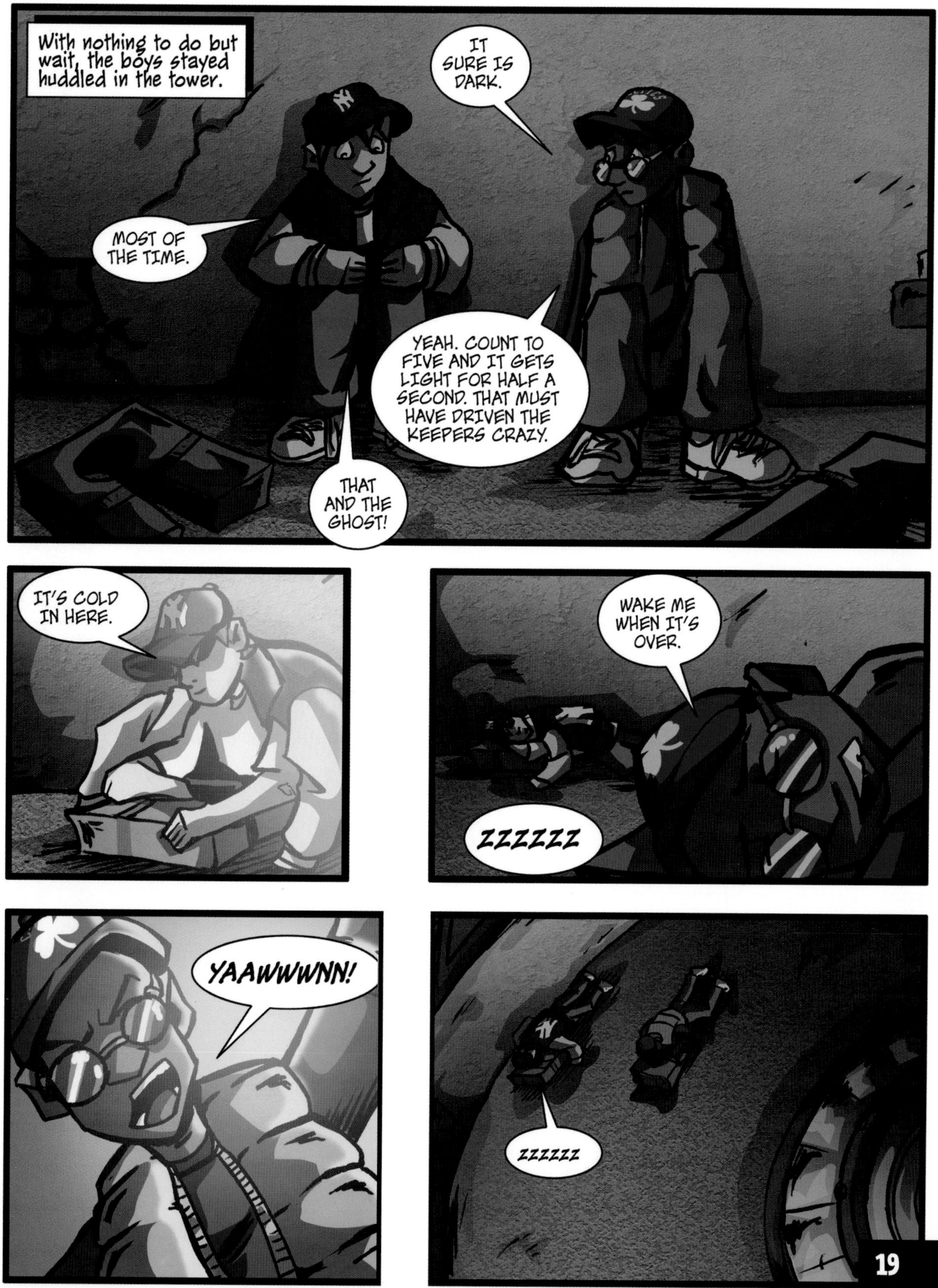

With nothing to do but wait, the boys stayed huddled in the tower.
IT SURE IS DARK.
MOST OF THE TIME.
YEAH. COUNT TO FIVE AND IT GETS LIGHT FOR HALF A SECOND. THAT MUST HAVE DRIVEN THE KEEPERS CRAZY.
THAT AND THE GHOST!
IT'S COLD IN HERE.
WAKE ME WHEN IT'S OVER.
ZZZZZZ
YAAWWWNN!
ZZZZZZ

The last resident lighthouse keeper lived on Bird Island in 1933. Very few people have slept there since.

KNOCK

KNOCK

KNOCK

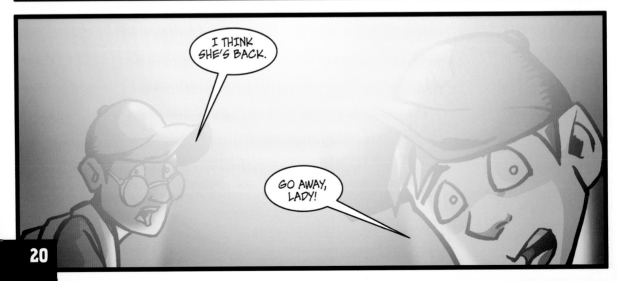

I THINK SHE'S BACK.

GO AWAY, LADY!

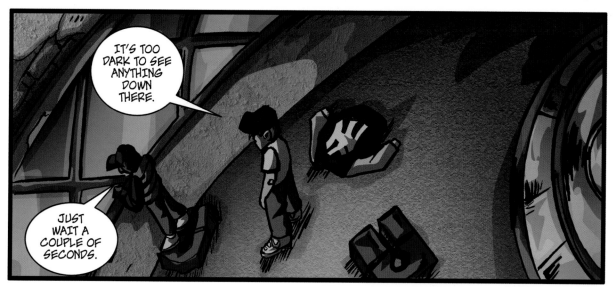

IT'S TOO DARK TO SEE ANYTHING DOWN THERE.

JUST WAIT A COUPLE OF SECONDS.

TOO BRIGHT.

IT'S LIKE BEING INSIDE A LIGHTBULB.

DID YOU SEE HER?

NO, BUT—

KNOCK

KNOCK

THERE'S YOUR ANSWER.

21

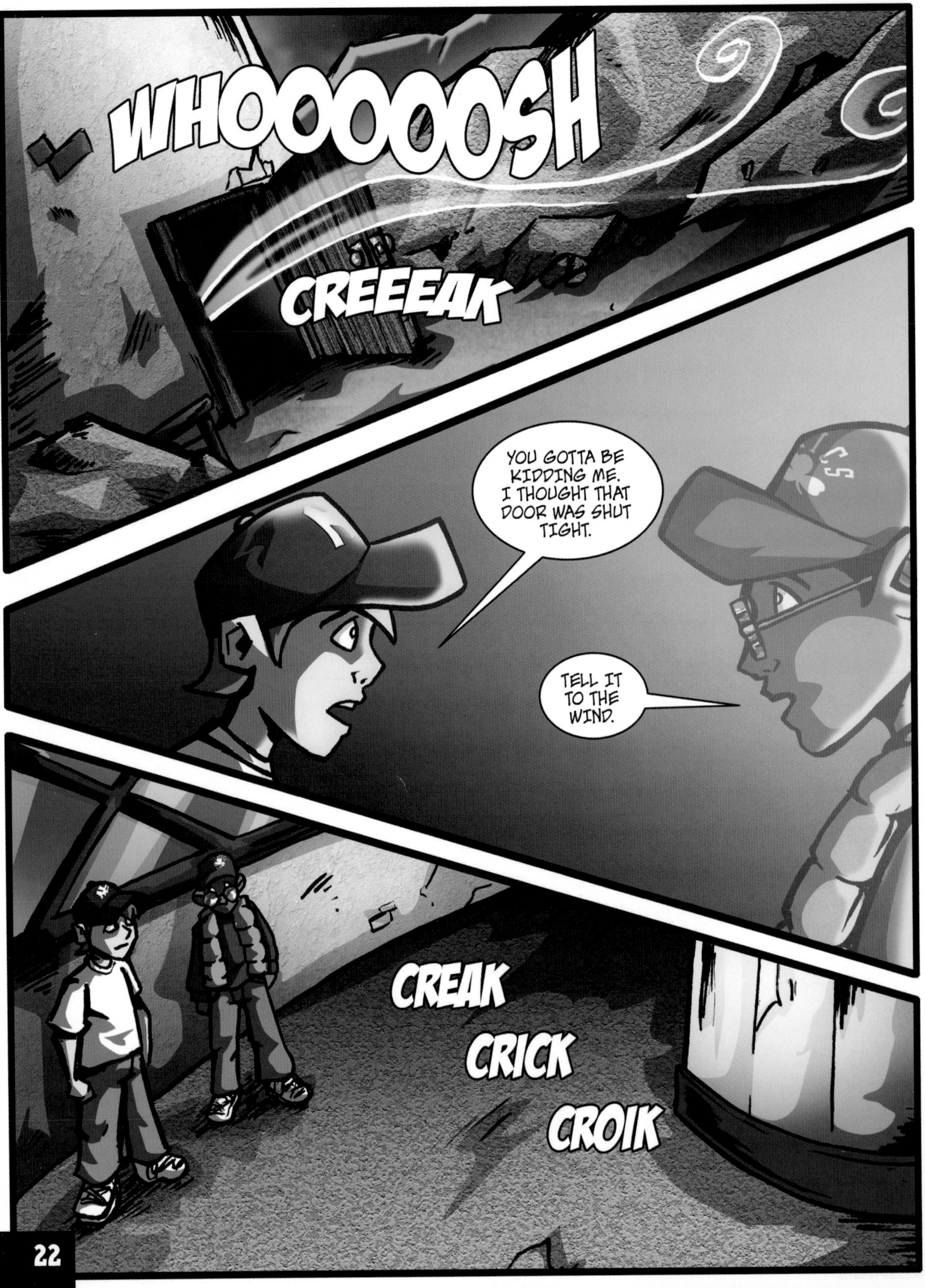
WHOOOOOOSH
CREEEAK
YOU GOTTA BE KIDDING ME. I THOUGHT THAT DOOR WAS SHUT TIGHT.
TELL IT TO THE WIND.
CREAK
CRICK
CROIK

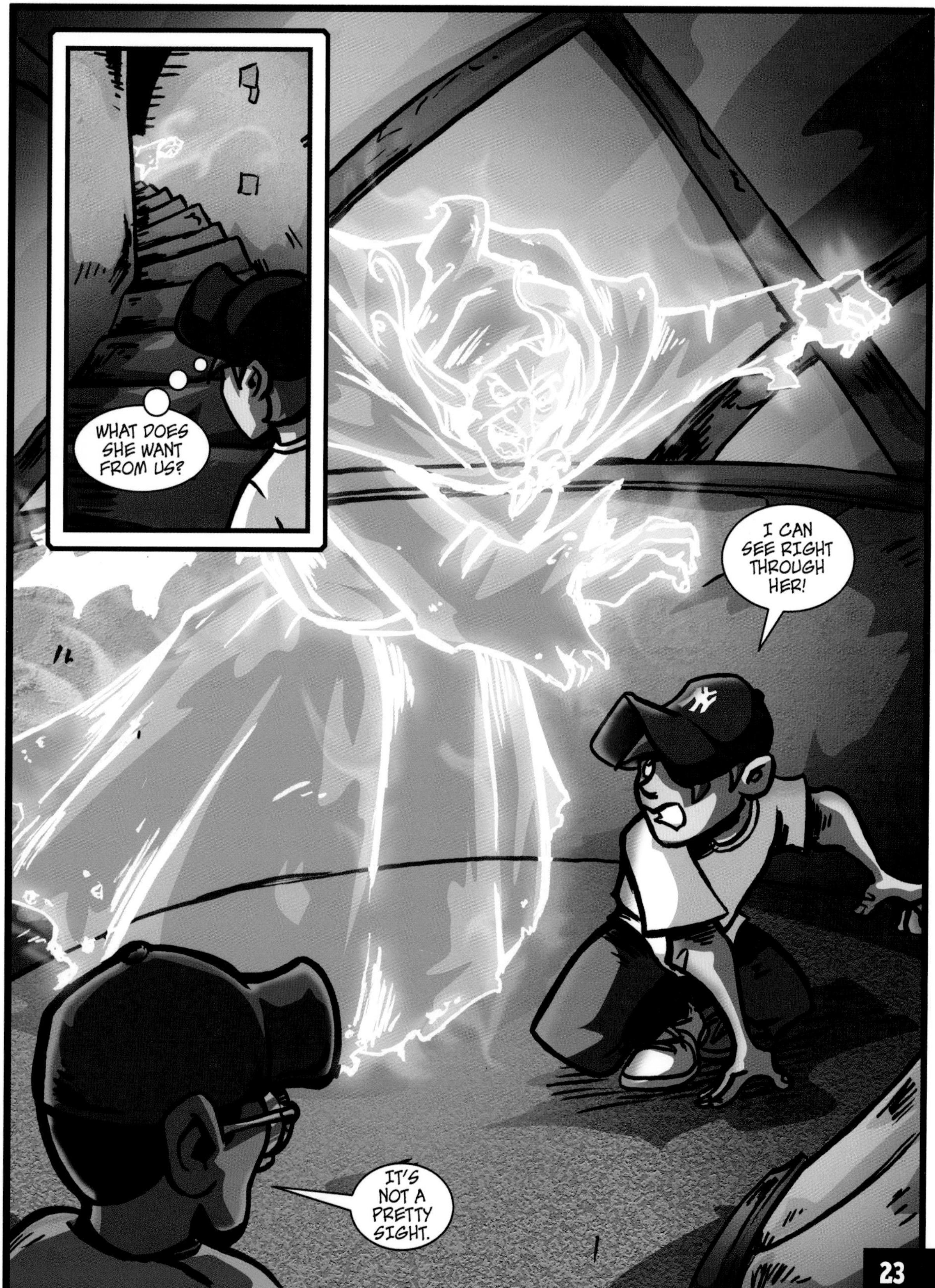
WHAT DOES SHE WANT FROM US?
I CAN SEE RIGHT THROUGH HER!
IT'S NOT A PRETTY SIGHT.

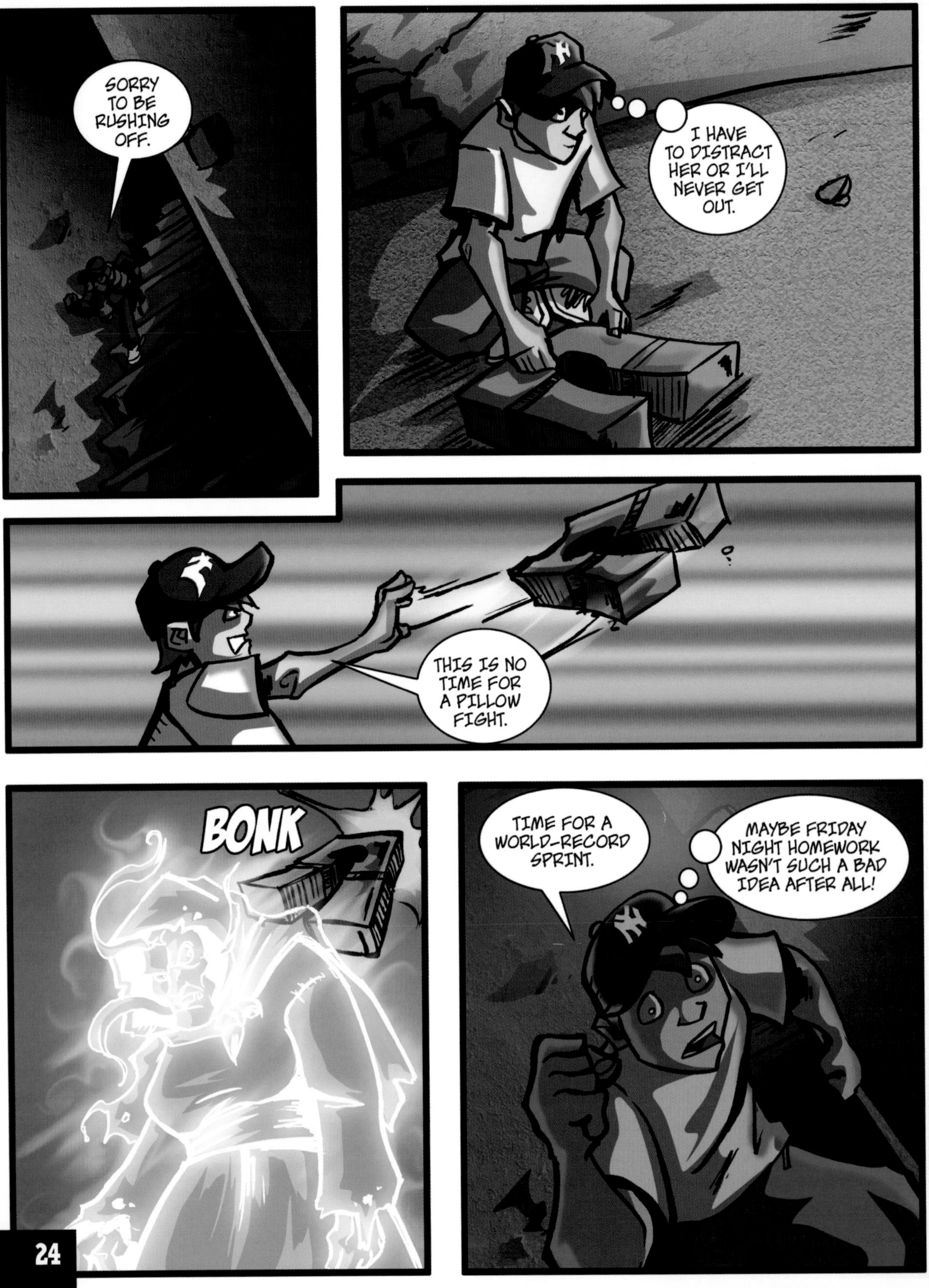
SORRY TO BE RUSHING OFF.
I HAVE TO DISTRACT HER OR I'LL NEVER GET OUT.
THIS IS NO TIME FOR A PILLOW FIGHT.
BONK
TIME FOR A WORLD-RECORD SPRINT.
MAYBE FRIDAY NIGHT HOMEWORK WASN'T SUCH A BAD IDEA AFTER ALL!

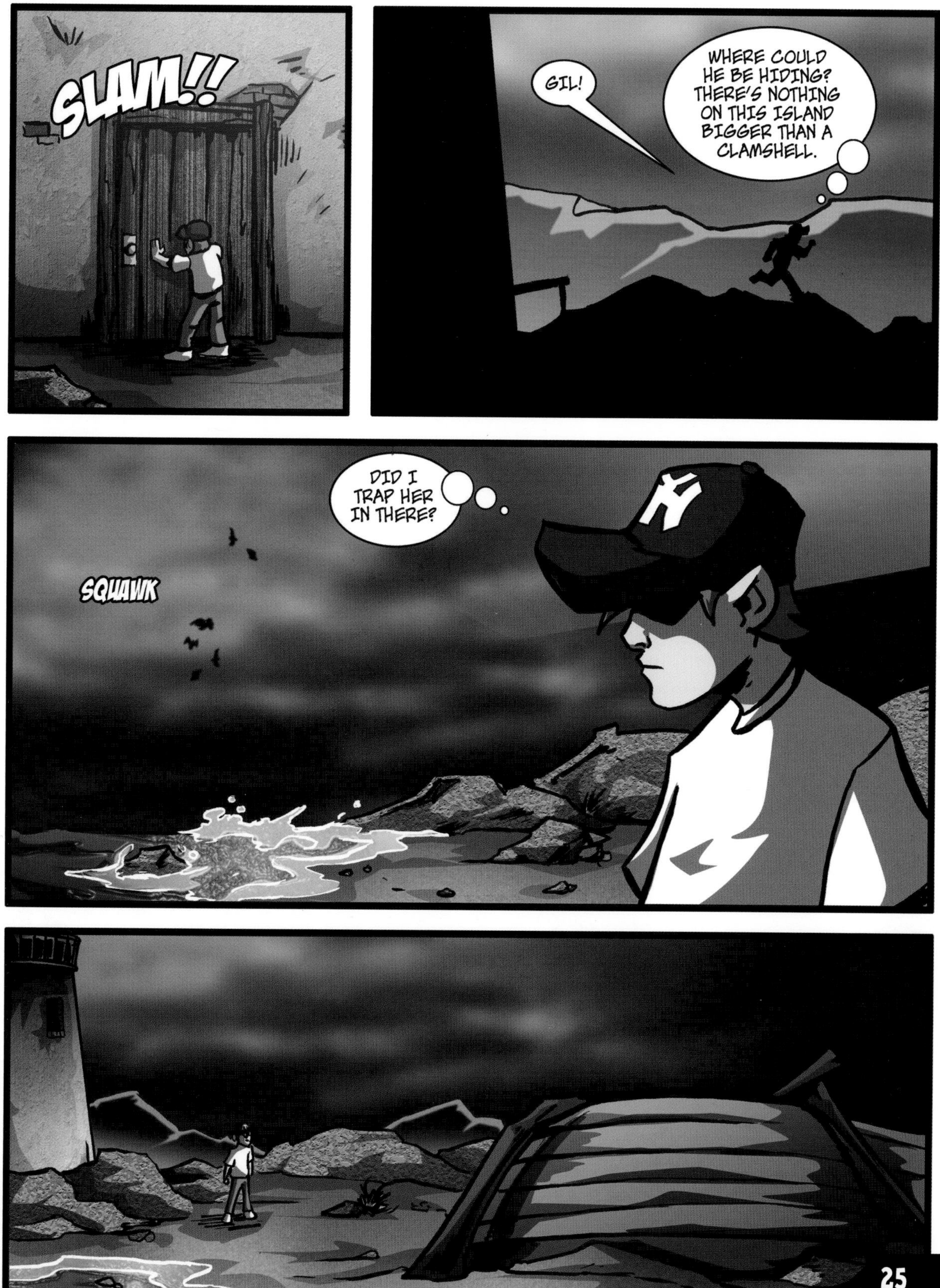
SLAM!!
GIL!
WHERE COULD HE BE HIDING? THERE'S NOTHING ON THIS ISLAND BIGGER THAN A CLAMSHELL.
DID I TRAP HER IN THERE?
SQUAWK

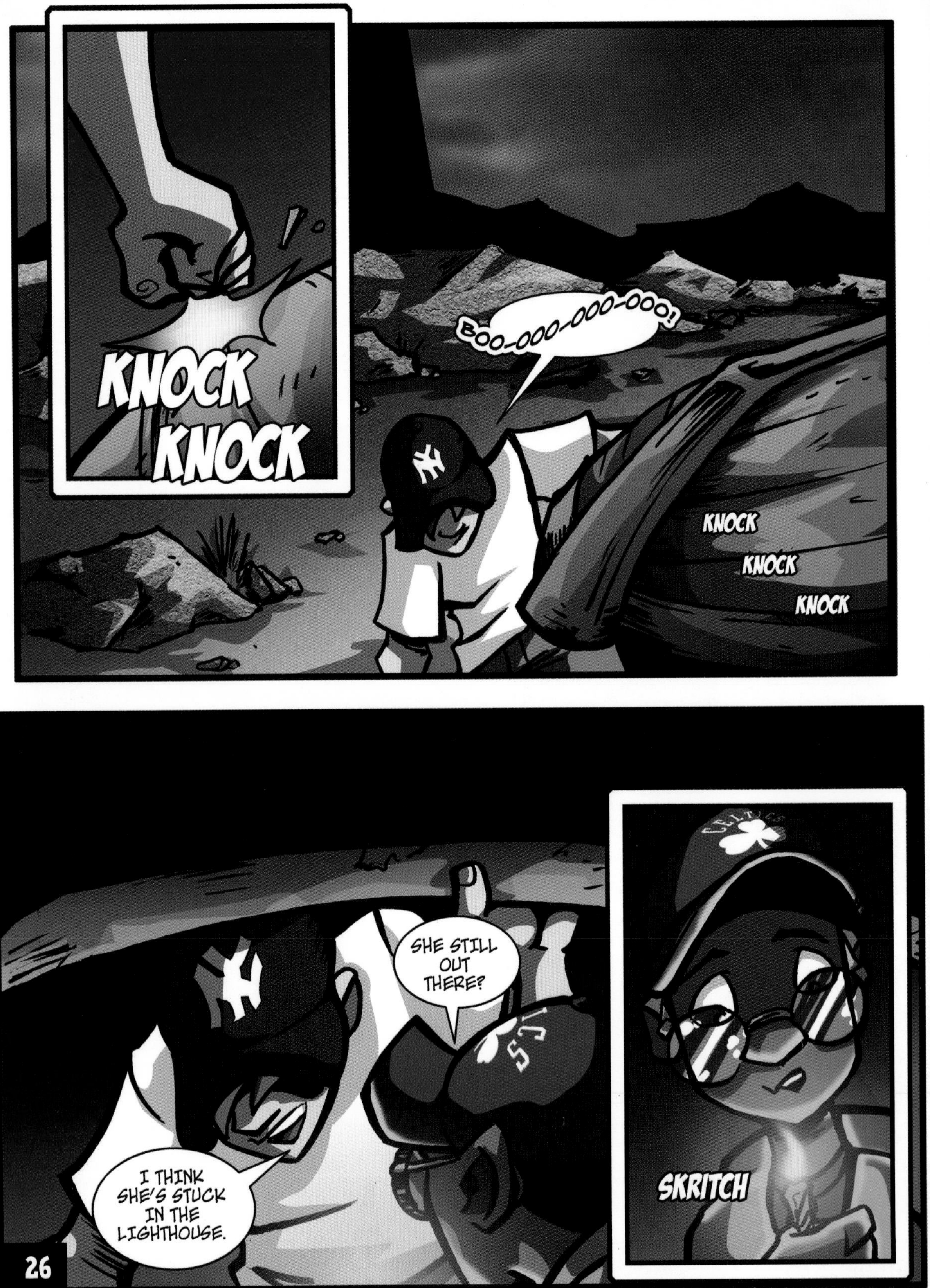
KNOCK
KNOCK
BOO-OOO-OOO-OOO!
KNOCK
KNOCK
KNOCK
SHE STILL OUT THERE?
I THINK SHE'S STUCK IN THE LIGHTHOUSE.
SKRITCH

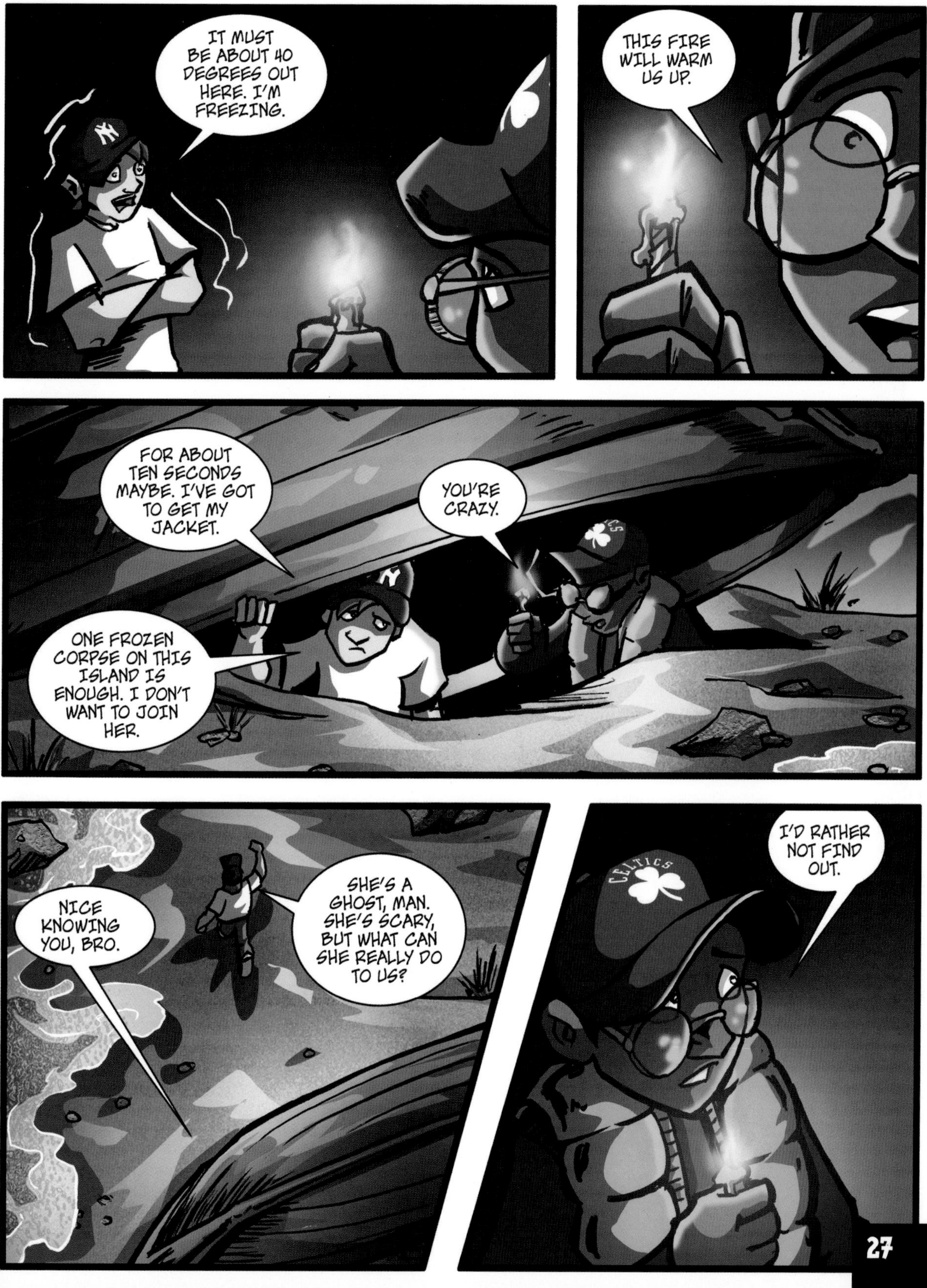
IT MUST BE ABOUT 40 DEGREES OUT HERE. I'M FREEZING.
THIS FIRE WILL WARM US UP.
FOR ABOUT TEN SECONDS MAYBE. I'VE GOT TO GET MY JACKET.
YOU'RE CRAZY.
ONE FROZEN CORPSE ON THIS ISLAND IS ENOUGH. I DON'T WANT TO JOIN HER.
SHE'S A GHOST, MAN. SHE'S SCARY, BUT WHAT CAN SHE REALLY DO TO US?
NICE KNOWING YOU, BRO.
I'D RATHER NOT FIND OUT.
CELTICS

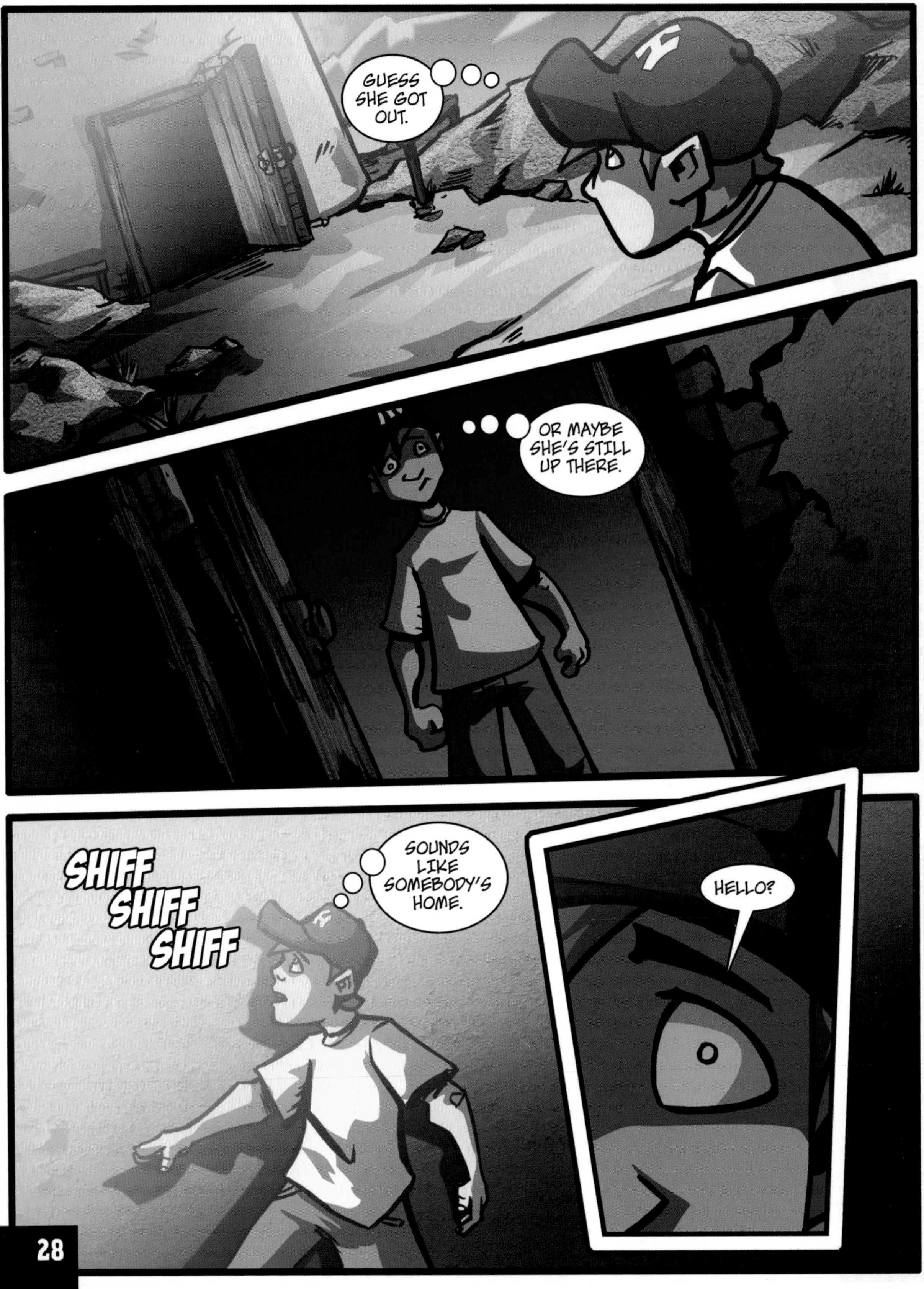
GUESS SHE GOT OUT.
OR MAYBE SHE'S STILL UP THERE.
SHIFF SHIFF SHIFF
SOUNDS LIKE SOMEBODY'S HOME.
HELLO?

I KNOW I DIDN'T HANG THAT UP THERE.

THE JACKET'S WARM FROM THAT LIGHT. THANKS, LADY, WHEREVER YOU ARE.

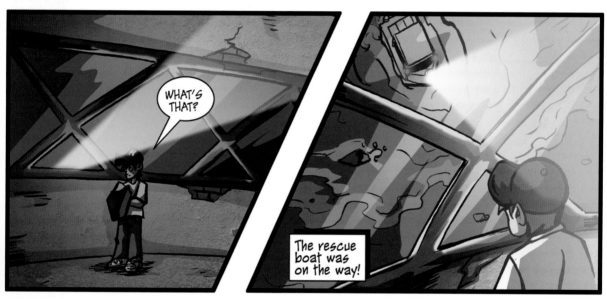

WHAT'S THAT?

The rescue boat was on the way!

GIL! THEY'RE COMING! GET OUT FROM UNDER THAT ROWBOAT!

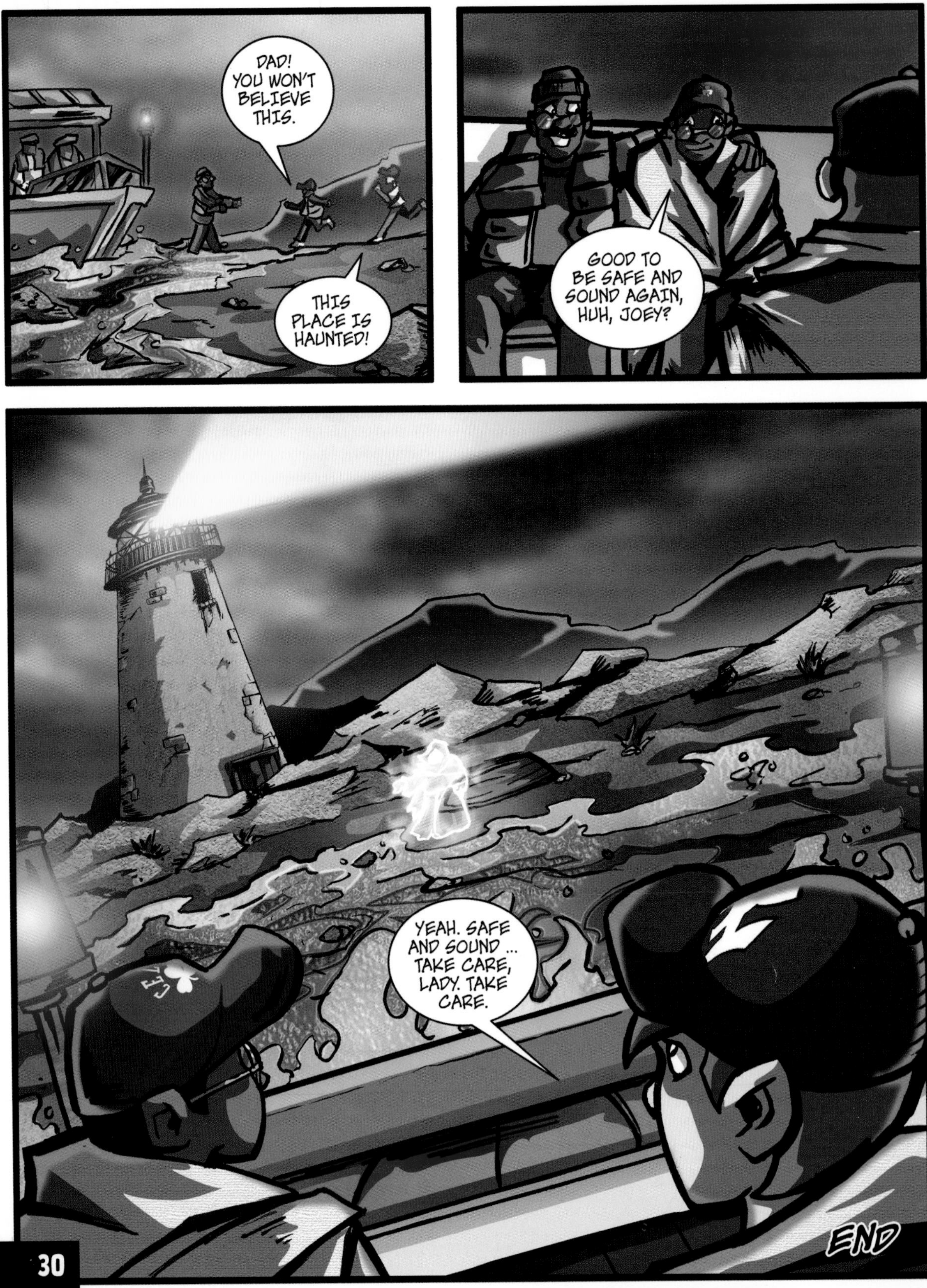
DAD! YOU WON'T BELIEVE THIS.
THIS PLACE IS HAUNTED!
GOOD TO BE SAFE AND SOUND AGAIN, HUH, JOEY?
YEAH. SAFE AND SOUND ... TAKE CARE, LADY. TAKE CARE.
END

THE BIRD ISLAND LIGHTHOUSE
(SIPPICAN HARBOR, BUZZARDS BAY, MA)

Although it is very small (less than two acres) Bird Island carries some tall stories in its history. The island's lighthouse opened in September 1819, and its first keeper was rumored to be a former pirate. Some said that the man, William S. Moore, was sent to the island as punishment for his crimes.

The lighthouse was badly damaged in a storm only three months after it opened. In a letter about the December 1819 storm, Moore wrote: "A very violent gale . . . has swept away every thing movable from the island; and among other things my boat."

The storm did not sweep away Moore's wife, but her life on the island was very difficult. Local residents reported that they could hear her cries from across the water.

Mrs. Moore died on the island and was buried there. Some reports said that her husband had murdered her. Others said that she died because he refused to take her to the mainland for medical treatment.

Regardless of how she died, many of the later lighthouse keepers claimed that she never really left. They said they could hear her knocking on the lighthouse door at night.

The Bird Island Lighthouse went out of service in 1933 and remained unused for more than 60 years. On July 4, 1997, the restored lighthouse was re-lighted. The unmanned solar-powered lighthouse continues to operate.

GLOSSARY

anchor - an object attached to a ship or boat by a cable and thrown overboard to hold it securely in a particular place.

bait - something, such as food, used to bring something to a hook or trap.

banished - to drive out or officially require someone to leave and never return.

corpse - the dead remains of a human or animal.

driftwood - wood that drifts on water or is washed ashore.

gale - a wind from 32 to 63 miles per hour (52 to 101 kmph).

solar power - using the sun's rays to create electricity.

tinder - something that easily catches fire.

WEB SITES

To learn more about Bird Island, visit ABDO Group online at **www.abdopublishing.com**. Web sites about the island are featured on our Book Links page. These links are routinely monitored and updated to provide the most current information available.